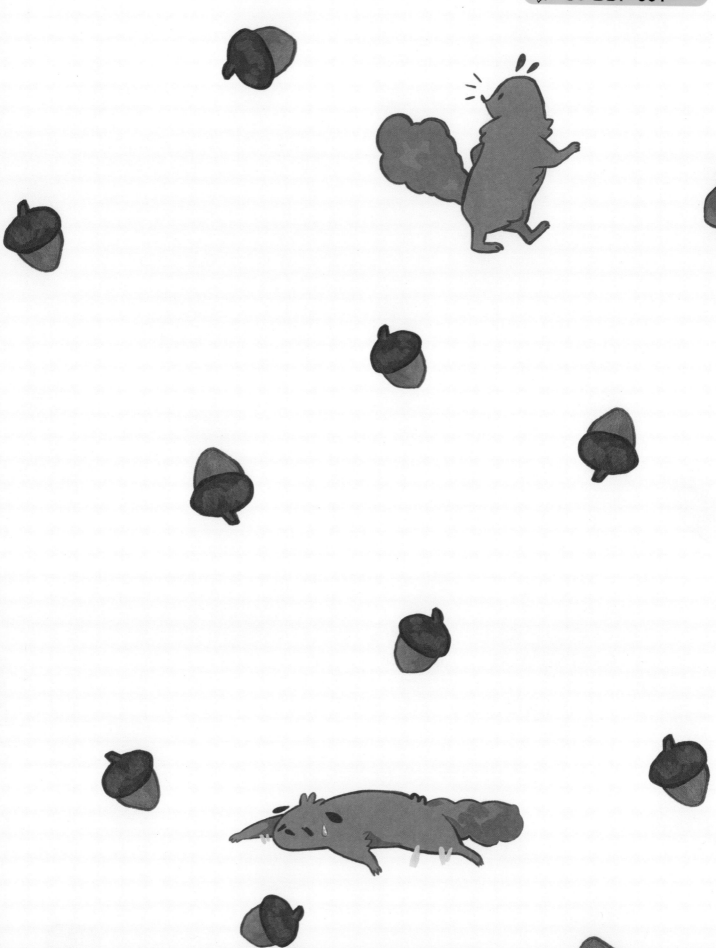

A SQUIRREL THRIVES

LET'S WRITE A STORY, MOMMY!

EMMEMM PUBLISHING
NEW YORK

SHE CLIMBED TO THE FIRST LIMB,
FELT HUNGRY.
CAME DOWN, GOT A NUT TO EAT AND ABANDONED THE CLIMB.

THE NEXT DAY...

THE SQUIRREL ATE A NUT,

STARTED THE CLIMB,

GOT TO THE SECOND LIMB,

BUT FELT THIRSTY.

SHE RAN RIGHT DOWN
AND DID NOT RETURN.

THE FOLLOWING DAY...

THE SQUIRREL CLUTCHED A NUT, GRABBED SOME WATER,

CLIMBED TO THE FIRST LIMB, PAUSED TO EAT AND DRINK,

THEN SPRINTED UP TWO MORE LIMBS.

SHE THOUGHT SHE HEARD A MOUNTAIN LION, MOMMY!

YES, SHE GOT SCARED AND SCAMPERED DOWN TO SAFETY.

THE SQUIRREL WAS BRAVE.

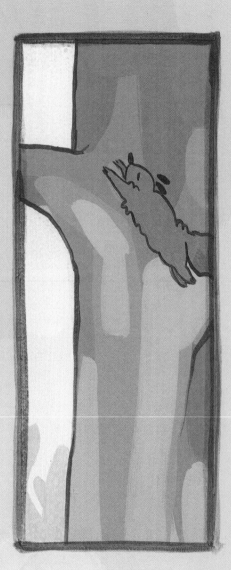

SHE HOPPED UP FROM ONE LIMB TO ANOTHER,

BUT HIT A SNAG WITH BROKEN LIMBS AND MISSING STEPS,

HESITATED A MOMENT, AND RETREATED RELUCTANTLY.

THE SQUIRREL NEEDED
TO FIND A WAY TO THE TOP.

SHE CLIMBED UP THE TREE, SWINGING MONKEY-BAR STYLE OVER THE MISSING LIMBS...

THE SQUIRREL DID PUSH-UPS AND BUILT UP HER MUSCLES.

BUT, SHE HAD TO PEE,

SO SHE CAME RIGHT DOWN THE TREE HOLDING ON TIGHT.

I DON'T KNOW HOW TO END THE STORY, BABY!

I KNOW, I KNOW, MOMMY!
THE SQUIRREL WAITED AND WAITED. SHE GREW AND GREW UNTIL

SHE GOT BIG ENOUGH TO CLIMB THE TREE
AND BE FRIENDS WITH THE SQUIRRELS AT THE TOP.
THE END!
STORIES DON'T END THAT WAY, BABY!

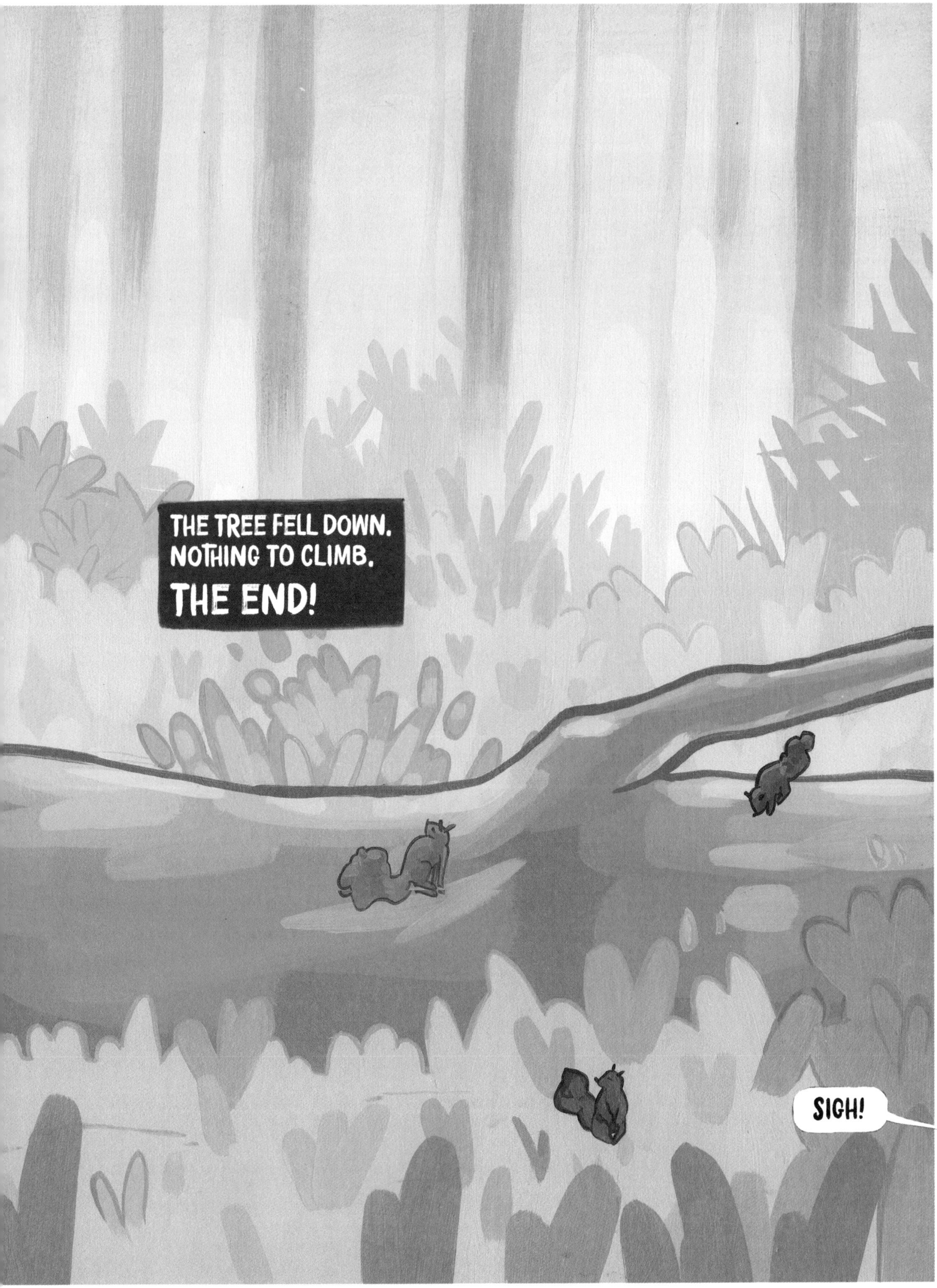
THE TREE FELL DOWN. NOTHING TO CLIMB. THE END!
SIGH!

A SMALL, FRESH, GREEN...

SIGH!

THIS IS NO FUN.
I AM THE ONLY ONE TELLING THE STORY, AND I AM THE ONE FIXING THE PROBLEMS.
YOU FINISH THE STORY, MOMMY!

THE SQUIRREL PRACTICED CLIMBING EACH DAY,

OVER AND OVER,

UNTIL SHE COULD SCURRY UP THE TREE IN ONE SPRINT.

ONCE YOU LEARN SOMETHING, THERE IS ALWAYS THE NEXT THING TO LEARN.

SHE TRIED TO HOP DOWN, MONKEY-BAR STYLE.

THE SQUIRREL HAD TO LEARN TO GET DOWN FROM THE TOP.

SHE TRIED TO SCRATCH HER WAY DOWN.

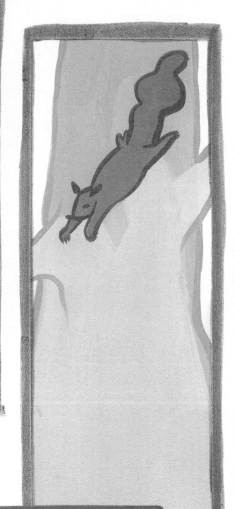

THEN SHE TRIED TO TIPTOE DOWN HEAD FIRST.

FINALLY SHE JUST RAN DOWN IN A THROBBING RUN.

ONE DAY, SHE PASSED A LITTLE SQUIRREL BY THE TREE.

SHE REMEMBERED HER SQUIRRELLY RIDE WHEN SHE WAS LITTLE, A LONG TIME AGO.

THE LITTLE SQUIRREL GOT TO
SEE THE WORLD FROM THE TOP
AND MAKE NEW FRIENDS.

THE END!

THE COLLABORATION

This story is a collaboration between Eira and her parents. When the family lived and hiked in Boulder Creek, CA, Eira asked to stop every few yards for snacks, water or because she said she was tired. Once challenged to a sprint or once she found a friend to join the hike, she was unstoppable.

This story came together first as an allegory of these hikes. Whenever the story got stuck, Eira proposed different ways to end it. Finally, she figured out that the story should be about learning to do things, and working hard to learn.

Amina proposed a graphic novel look for illustrating the book because each page had a sequence of actions. Also, it seemed a good challenge for the children to learn the language of graphic novels early. The squirrel had to be worked and reworked through collaboration. The family had to learn to be patient, collaborating over a year, until they could finally hold a copy of the book in their hands.

THE ARTIST

Amina Akhmadeeva is a New York City based illustrator
and currently attends the School of Visual Arts. She is set to graduate in
2020. With her passion for art, she aims to bring life to characters and
narratives. She is a proud owner of a cat and many plants.

aminaillustration.com

THE PUBLISHER

Emmemm Publishing, LLC., produces children's books that are true
collaborations between grownups and children, and that incorporate
innovative multidimensional art. Each book is borne out of many family
conversations. The hope is that reading these books will lead to many
discussions that stir readers to personalize the narrative and experiment
with the art. With such projects, the child will grow with books while
books and stories will grow with the child.

emmemmpublishing.com

Published by
Emmemm Publishing, LLC.
1732 1st Ave #20752
New York, NY 10128
emmemmpublishing.com

A Squirrel Thrives
Text: Eira Muthu (Eira), S. Muthukrishnan (Muthu)
and Vladimira Jakubikova (Vlada)
Art: Amina Akhmadeeva
Book design: Martina Rozinajova
Printed in Czech Republic by Protisk s. r. o.
Library of Congress Control Number: 2019902710
ISBN-13: 978-0-9995533-4-3